Seven Day Wonder

Seven Day Wonder

Sensual Romance by

Lana Lundon

A Seven Day Wonder is a person or a process supposedly perfected in only seven days.
—Quoted from the Free Dictionary

The most tantalizing fantasies lurk within the deepest recesses of our minds. When the urges demand release, we must set them free.

—LL

Thus the birth of Seven Day Wonder. I unlocked my demons, permitting them to roam the pages of this book with their erotic persuasion. I hope you enjoy the world *they* have created.

The Arrival

"Your knuckles were turning white back there." She reaches over the console, trickles her fingers down my arm, then plucks the flannel sleeve of the shirt I'm wearing under my down vest. "Broke out the hunting gear, I see."

I hear a bubble pop through her ruby lips and when my eyes flash over her face, she's chomping gum, grinning, grooving to Lady Gaga.

Hair lustrous with sunshine filtering through the window, Johanna is radiant.

I lower the radio. Make my face serious. My voice deep. "Yeah. I plan on hunting for the next seven days." I snatch her hand, bring it to my lips. "You." I nibble her fingers and grunt like an animal. "I finally have you all to myself, woman." I shoot her a toothy grin. "Without commercial interruption."

"You're nutty." She giggles. Scrubs her soft palm over my stubbly cheek, cups my chin, then tugs on my bottom lip. "I thought you shaved this morning."

"I did. You bring out the hairy beast in me. What can I say?" I mouth a kiss as her hand slips away.

I pull my eyes from the road to steal another heart-stopping glimpse of Johanna. I still can't believe the girl sitting beside me is mine. She's ten years my junior, and sometimes I wonder how long we'll be able to keep up this pace. Careers. Nightlife. Cock-blowing romance.

Ten years doesn't seem like a big deal when a guy's thirty-six, but how about twenty or thirty years down the road? When my crow's feet are sprouting crow's feet, and she's still a runway-ready knockout. Athletic women like Johanna age better than hard-living guys like me, who have been on the streets since their teens, scrapping their way through life.

I shake my head. A laugh rumbles under my breath. At least I'll never go soft. When I'm around Johanna, my hormones rage like the storm the weatherman predicted. The fire she stirs is something even age won't eradicate. A blizzard might enhance it though. I'm about to show her the real me.

I glance at the sky. It's clear blue for as far as eye can see. "So much for the airline's threat to cancel our flight."

She pops another bubble. "Seriously. I know how much you've been looking forward to this trip."

"And you haven't been?"

"Of course I have, but getting away at this time of year isn't easy."

"Yeah. I guess we're both ridiculously tied to our jobs." I shake my head. "We should rob a boat, sail to parts unknown. Live on fish, fruit, and sex."

"Don't tempt me. Thinking about what I'll be returning to makes castaway a very attractive alternative." She sighs.

"What's wrong, babe? They overworking you?"

She hesitates. Clears her throat. I know that muffled sound which is usually accompanied by pursed lips. The wheels are turning in her beautiful head. She's trying to be evasive without triggering my curiosity. "Nothing I can't handle."

From the corner of my eye, I see her take a handful of tissues from her satchel, wipe weeping vapor off her side window and gaze out. I imagine she sees the same things I'm seeing. Or maybe she's looking past the snow covered fences and evergreens dressing both sides of the road. The fields of bare trunks, icy streams, more snow, and wilderness.

"You know I'm here, honey. If you need

muscle." I grab her hand and squeeze. "Nobody messes with my baby."

Her grip tightens on mine. "Office politics, that's all. Nothing to worry about."

She doesn't sound very convincing ... My stomach dives.

After a cloverleaf turn, the double lane highway disappears from my rear view mirror.

"Now that we're out of heavy traffic, I can relax." I reach over and tweak her full breast which is covered by a soft, v-neck sweater. Her cleavage holds my attention, my touch. I have a hard time concentrating on the country road.

They say smartphones are addictive and cause accidents. Johanna is *my* addiction. I gesture to a road sign trimmed with snow that looks like fur. "Steep and winding incline. Slow." I chuckle. "I couldn't speed if I was running from the law."

She laughs. I turn to see her relax into her seat.

The engine is straining, hauling our vehicle up the side of the mountain with a pulley effect. "There's the lodge up ahead. Excited?"

The hideaway we're aiming for looks like a snapshot of the wild west, but the rustic structures are in stellar shape. Lots of windows. Strings of colorful lights crossing a narrow road. Lighted trees. An intimate settlement nestled at the foot of a towering range of mountains.

She sucks in a breath. "Oh my God, it's beautiful." She pulls my hand to her lips and rakes her teeth over my knuckles. "Yup. We're going to have a fantastic time."

After one last squeeze of her supple flesh, I wrap both palms around the steering wheel. "So it's gonna be *that* kind of trip, huh?" My jeaned crotch grows uncomfortably tight. My stomach bottoms out.

"Oh yeah. Biting ... clawing, and a lot of other good stuff." I hear the mischief in her voice, underlying desire. Feel the heat of her eyes watching for my reaction to her sexy, teasing tone.

I gulp down a swallow, feeling the way I did when I made my first collar. Gut tightening anticipation, followed by a rush. Thinking of the sendoff I got from the guys in the precinct when they heard I was taking Johanna to this resort, I chuckle.

"One of the boys threw an extra pair of cuffs into my bag." I squeeze her knee then drag my hand up her leg until it hits her crotch, my thumb zeroing in on her knit-covered clit. She stiffens, then eases into my palm. "Did you bring the toys?" At the thought, my cock tries to jerk, but my jeans restrain it.

"Of course I brought the toys. And no cop talk," she warns, her hand sliding along my thigh. "We're here for a restful getaway, remember? Just you and me, leaving our jobs and worries behind."

"Hmm. Restful. Are you telling me we can't have sex?"

She grabs a fistful of hair at the back of my head and tugs. "I never said we couldn't exercise."

"Keep it up." I tease. "Before the clock strikes three, those sexy clothes will be ripped off your body which I will work until you cry for mercy. That will be your punishment for dangling temptation under my nose and not letting me touch you."

"On the plane? Sandwiched between an elderly woman and two wide-eyed kids?" She laughs. "I don't know, Deck. You are a dirty old man."

"Dirty, yes. And if you're equating age to experience with that comment, you have no idea what you're in for, little girl."

She widens the gap in her thighs, plastering my hand against her folds. "Neither do you."

I shift in my seat. "You're killing me, babe. Thank Christ we're here is all I have to say."

She shakes her head and laughs. "You've got a one track mind."

"You ain't seen nothing yet, baby girl. This fresh air is invigorating."

"And my panties are getting wet." She reaches across the seat and plants a kiss on my cheek. "I'm so glad we came. We're gonna have an amazing time. Maybe we'll even extend our stay, huh." Her perfectly shaped brow shoots up.

"Now you're talking my language."

Our SUV climbs the plowed driveway, and in minutes we're parked in the lot. While Johanna slams the door and skips ahead, I shoulder our bags. "I like that truck," I call to the long bouncing curls at the back of her head. "Maybe I'll buy us one when we get home."

"Sure. And the lotto ticket I bought before we left this morning is going to be a winner, too." She laughs. "Come on old man. Let's get a move on. I'm hungry."

"Rub it in," I grumble.

"Oh I will. Brought the oils too." She stops long enough to whirl and wink.

"Turn around you. I like watching your ass when you walk. That short jacket gives me a bird's eye view of those pumping cheeks. Mmm. Gonna bite me some of them."

She pauses long enough to bend over and palm her butt. "You like my ass better than my face?" In a sneak attack, she fills her glove with hard packed snow blowers have piled beside the path. Without aiming, she nails the center of my chest. Then she breaks into laughter and runs.

I lurch into a jog. "Wait until I get my hands on you." Lugging the bags and laughing, I'm gasping, and my eyes are watering.

She breathlessly pulls ahead of me. "Never happen. I run track."

"And I ace endurance tests and catch bad guys. You're screwed."

"Mmm. I like the sound of that," she tosses over her shoulder.

By the time I catch my breath, she's standing at the double glass entry doors, grinning, waving.

Checking In

The desk clerk's eyes lock on Johanna. I shoot him a slow-spreading grin to tip him off: I'm the lucky bastard who gets to fuck her, buddy. Look but don't dare try to touch. Oh, and yeah, drooling is permitted. My sly grin spreads into a proud smile as he slides the key cards to our suite across the glossy counter.

"Have a nice stay." His startled gaze darts from Johanna to me. There's a silent communication between us; a guy thing. I'm a jungle animal defending my turf, and he's backed off.

"Oh we plan on it, believe me." I wink and nod.

We take the elevator to the top floor. Johanna

is ogling the blue and gold carpet running the length of the wide corridors.

"The inside of this lodge is nothing like the exterior. I figured we'd be bunking with the horses."

As our suite is on the top floor, the ceilings are vaulted. "It cost enough. It should be posh. Do you think I'd bring you to a stable?"

"I don't care where I am, as long as I'm with you." She hugs my arm, pressing into my side.

I slip the key through the slot, push the door open, drop the bags and sweep Johanna off her feet.

"What are you doing?" She giggles.

"What does it look like I'm doing. Carrying you over the threshold." My lips reach for hers.

"Is that a proposal?"

The tips of our noses touch. I inhale her sweet breath. "Would you want it to be?" I've become swept away. The conversation is suddenly as serious as my face feels, hers looks. We both stiffen. I set her on the heels of her boots, retrieve the bags and kick the door closed.

"This is some nice shack." I scan the room, admiring the plush red carpeting, nappy white sofas set before the fieldstone fireplace. My eyes settle on the open bedroom door, then roam down the hall to the bathroom. "I might just hop into that shower. Care to join me?"

Johanna doesn't reply because she's off in another direction, exploring. I watch her high, tight ass sway as she saunters to the wall of windows, gazes out and marvels at the view.

"It's barely Halloween and they're already decorating for New Year's." She clicks her tongue.

"Holidays are big biz up here, sweetie." I come up behind her, wind my arms around her waist, nuzzle her neck. "Mmm. You smell good, taste better." I run my palms over the front of her fuzzy pink sweater, cupping her breasts.

Her breath whispers a brief sigh and her body relaxes against mine.

I slip my hands under her sweater, up and over the smooth cups of her demi bra, my fingertips tracing her cleavage. My palms draw circles around her ripening nipples, and her next sigh is heavier. She lifts her arms, tightens them around my neck and laces her fingers. The arch of her back forces her breasts deeper into my palms.

I press my hardness against her ass. My chin tunnels beneath the shoulder of her sweater, my lips nipping her velvet skin. "You have the greatest breasts," I whisper, cupping, massaging. My thumbs circle her hard nipples that are digging through the lacy fabric.

I swallow the drool gathering at the corners of my mouth. With one swipe, I lift the sweater up and over her head. Her static mane catches rays of afternoon sun and champagne blends with spirals of silver threading.

I find the delicate clasp and with two fingers, set her breasts free. Without the support of her bra, her breasts bounce deliciously into my palms. I knead for a sensational minute, then pinch her nipples. She strains against me, resting the back of her head on my shoulder, sighs turning to moans. Her nipples are so erect, I'm ready to ravage them. My fingers press harder and twist. Her hips rock and her ass massages my erection, which is throbbing in time with my heart.

"What's going through your head right now?"

"I'm aching. I want you inside me." Her voice is husky.

"Tell me how you feel at this very minute."

"Wet."

"How wet?" My chin rests on her shoulder, which I swipe with lazy strokes of my tongue.

"My pants are soaked." She grabs one of my hands. "Feel for yourself."

"Not yet." Hunger for her makes me hoarse.

When I spin her, she stares up at me, her expression drunk, which triggers my lust even more. I lower my face and capture a breast at a time, sucking lightly, flicking my tongue. "How about now?" I lift my face, stare into her drowsy eyes.

"Horny as hell," she murmurs. "Strip." She reaches for me.

I lower her arms. "Not me. You."

"Pretty demanding, aren't we." Her heavy lids are lifted by her arching brows. Blinking up at me, she chews her bottom lip. Threads her fingers through my hair. "What do you have in mind, officer?"

I watch her neck, the movement of her throat as she swallows. My throat feels the same. Constricted with longing. "Detective. And what did I just tell you to do?" I narrow my eyes.

When she says, "Strip," the breath she exhales reaches my face.

"That's right. Now you're catching on." I free her long enough for her to slide out of her pants. When they drop to the carpet, she kicks them away. "No cheating. Panties too." My voice is gruff, as though I'm dealing with a suspect I've just arrested.

She stares up at me, eyelids fluttering.

"Don't give me the eyes. Drop your panties." I slide a finger across the wet fabric covering her crotch. "That's an order."

She slips her thumbs under the elastic, bends at the waist, and peels them slowly down her shapely legs.

"You've got moves like a stripper." Watching the sultry shifts of her body, the yearning expression on her face, I fight the urge to throw her over my shoulder, lay her on the floor, and fuck her brains out.

"In a little while, I'm going to toss you on that sofa, lift your ankles, drag your ass to the edge of the cushions, and spread your legs." I haul in a tortured breath. "Would you like that?"

"Yes."

"Yes who?"

"Yes officer."

"Detective," I wheeze. "I'm going to ease into you nice and slow, then pound your pussy like a madman. Because you're driving me insane." Perspiration dampens my hairline. I want her so bad my balls ache, but what I have in mind takes control. Time.

"Move away from the window."

"To where?"

"That wall over there." I gesture to the corner of the room, which is falling into shadows, and watch her bare ass wiggle as the soles of her feet skim the carpet. She's as graceful as a dancer. Her silhouette is luscious: rounded hips, perky breasts, projectile nipples. My dick throbs harder.

"Back against the wall. No quick moves. Just nice and slow and sexy." I plaster her arms to her sides, palms flat against her thighs. "Hands stay right here. Understand? Or do I have to cuff you."

She swallows hard and nods. "Don't cuff me yet." Her gaze hits the painful bulge throbbing between my legs. I have a feeling she wants her hands on me. Holy shit, do I want her hands on me. "I promise I won't move." She rolls her bottom lip under her very white front teeth.

"When you need something to lean on ..." I drag a nearby chair to her side. "When you can't take anymore, and your legs start to buckle, you can hold onto this. Other than that, don't move a muscle ... not yet."

Her cheeks flush. The tip of her tongue brushes

her lips, then her mouth spreads with a smile. I watch the rise and fall of those tantalizing breasts, lay my hand over her heart, feel its demanding beat. Right now, mine is skipping beats.

"Your skin is breaking out in goose bumps. What should I do about it?"

"Mmm." She lifts her chin. Closes her eyes. "Lick it."

I lower my face and oblige. When my tongue rolls across her chest, laps her breasts, her body shifts and strains.

I pull my lips away, bringing a nipple with me, making a popping sound as I release the expanding bud. "Enough of that. Ready for something else?"

She nods.

I circle her belly with my fingertips, glide over her abs and cup her breasts with my working man's palms. "You're so beautiful," I murmur, struggling to control my pulse. My erection. "And you're going to come for me while we just stand here." Her face is tense. Her eyelids are sealed. "Look at me." I reach between her legs, tweak her clit. When my fingers come away, they're wet, sticky. "Got it?"

She chews her bottom lip again and nods. "This is getting interesting." She looks stoned, then her features melt with desire. Her breath catches in her throat, so I know she's struggling along with me.

My eyes burn into hers. My tongue slowly

swipes my bottom lip. I strum her nipples. Twist them. When she sucks in a moan, I hold the pressure. "How does this feel?"

"Delicious."

"Describe the delicious."

"It's an incredible sensation." Her lips twitch. "My body is tingling ... all over. Pulsing with jolts of electricity." She tenses. Her words come with small gasps. "I'm on the verge of an orgasm."

"I'll tell you when to come." I pinch her nipples harder, twist more aggressively. "And now?"

Her head rolls from side to side. Her long hair tangles, loose strands falling across her face, clinging to her shoulders. I watch perspiration gather and trickle down the already moist valley between her breasts. Her eyes beg. She reaches for my hand.

"Nah ah. No touching."

With the onset of rapture, her features freeze with pain, her jaw clenches. Once more, she attempts to bring one of my hands to her crotch, but I strangle her wrist. "Nuh uh. You're going to do this alone. With me just watching, tweaking. Bathing your nipples with my long, wet tongue. My hot breath blowing on them. This is how it's going to happen. Understand?"

The grip of her lips loosens with a curse. She moans, throws back her head and clenches her thighs. "Use your muscles," I growl shifting my weight because my dick wants to spring through my fly.

Her eyelids flutter then close. Her face pulls into a tortured expression. She brings a finger to her mouth and bites down. I tear my eyes from her face to watch her thighs clasp shut and slide with a cock-raising rhythm. Her hips roll, then buck.

"Look at me," I command.

Her lids snap open. With a guttural cry, she slumps against the wall, hips writhing wildly, then slowing to a sensual beat all her own.

"Now you can come." I squeeze her breasts together, lower my lips, and suck her nipples until she screams.

"Deck ..." Along with a groan, she chokes out my name. "I can't stand it anymore. You've got to ..."

"Fuck you?"

"Yes."

"Say it."

"I want you inside me. Now. Or I think I'll die." She chews her slackened lower lip so hard, I'm afraid it will bleed. Her eyes plead as she whispers, "Please ..."

By now, my legs are buckling. We sink to the floor where I stretch out her limbs, position her body precisely. I brace on an elbow. Suck on her lips. With two fingers and a thumb, work her passion until I bring her to another screeching orgasm.

Something inhuman brews inside my heat. I

doubt I've ever been this hard. My heart is thudding out of my chest, my mouth is literally foaming. The lump in my jeans is growing larger, while the one in my throat is prohibiting my swallowing.

I graze her breasts with my teeth, lick my way down her ribs, slide my fingers in and out rhythmically, circling her clit with the pad of my thumb. Spread her legs wide enough for my head, douse her with my tongue.

"I can't take anymore." Thrusting her hips, she groans. Fists my hair and screams. The air fills with labored breathing, then she goes limp, and I'm cradling her against my chest. Brushing back her tangled hair.

"How many times did you come?" I don't have to make my voice husky. I couldn't sound normal right now if I tried. I'm in another world. Barely able to think. I run my fingers over her plump folds. Drop kisses on her neck and face.

"I lost count. You have million dollar lips, baby," she pants. "And fingers. I never knew I could come with you just sucking my breasts. Staring at me with that look in your eyes."

"What kind of look?"

"Like a starving animal. Like you wanted to tear me apart."

"I do. But I'm gonna take you slow. Slip into your slick little pussy and barely move. Make you suffer. Beg me to slam into you. Fuck you in so many positions your throat will be raw from screaming. They'll be pounding on our door, because they'll think someone's being murdered in here."

She plucks my chin. Draws my face to hers and murmurs directly into my mouth as her lips cover mine. "I'm gonna curl your toes, detective."

"Back against that sofa. Sit up straight." She drags my sweater over my head. Grabs a fistful of my hair and jerks my head back. Sucks on the side of my neck. Bites my nipples. She squeezes my balls. "Stretch out."

"I ..."

"Shut up, officer. I'm in control now. Do you understand?"

"I can't argue with a lady." My smile is as weak as my limbs.

She tugs my jeans to my ankles, then she's on her knees, fingers sliding, lips following. Sucking the bulging head, whipping it with her tongue. "You're gonna make me come," I gasp. "Before I even make it inside."

Her grip tightens. She lifts her head, lips massaging my throbbing shaft. "Where's your self control, detective ..." she purrs.

"Wise ass," I mumble under my breath. When my overheated head hits the back of her throat, I ease her away. My heart is thumping, beating erratically. I think I'm about to have a coronary. "I can see the headline news. Detective croaks while fucking his sarcastic girlfriend." I try to put my mind in another place, joke my way out of coming. "I want to fuck you right now. So bad. In the shower. Under cool water."

She shoots me a brow, then a sexy grin.

I nod. "Yeah. I need something to cool down. You're too fucking hot to handle."

"So handle me then, in the shower." She's on her feet, pulling me to mine.

I throw my arms around her waist, grip her ass and back her down the hall, sucking her neck the entire time.

We all but fall through the doorway, her giggling, me trying to hold it together. "Let me test the waters." I wink. Slap her ass.

She pauses beside me, pulls her messy hair onto the top of her head, rubs the back of her neck and checks out the bathroom. Her gaze falls on the whirlpool tub. I know this because mine is taking the same direction.

Her body glistens with perspiration. I don't know what to touch first. I want to devour every inch of her. Inside and out. Christ, how much more breath can she suck from my lungs?

I press my temples. "Shower first. Tub next." I run a finger between her breasts and down her tummy, lingering on the moisture inside her swelling. I tweak her clit and watch another outbreak of goose bumps erupt upon her skin.

I lift her chin, bring her lips to mine. "Baby, this is going to be the best seven days of my life."

She traces my jaw line with the fingertips of one hand. Grabs my sack with the other and grins.

"Mine too."

I fix the temp, then step beneath the strong stream of water. Close my eyes and lift my face. Douse my hair, my throbbing erection. It feels so cool, refreshing. From the corner of my eye, I glimpse Johanna, standing like a beautiful statue, arms over her head, breasts alert, tummy flat and toned. Her nipples are rosy pink and swollen, like her mouth, her pussy. I swallow a mouthful of shower. My dick slaps my belly.

"Invite me in?" She arches her brows and reaches for my sack. My eyes follow her hand, drop to her arched foot, her pointed toe. Lifting my gaze, I lick my lips. Browse her legs. Linger on the puckered blood filled lips between her slightly spread thighs. I'm heart-pounding, gasping for air.

"You're killing me. Come here." I grab her hands and yank her in beside me.

While I crush her in my arms, our lips seal in an amazing, tongue-sucking kiss. I slam her back against the wet tiles, press my hardness into her belly. She reaches between us, slides her fingers up and down my slippery shaft.

"I'm so ready to ride you."

"No condom?" I whisper against her neck.

"No condom. I started the Pill ..."

Her fingers grab a hunk of my wet hair. She rocks her hips against mine, claws my back with her sharp fingernails.

I lick water from her wet breasts, suck droplets off her nipples, while my fingers work between her folds.

She shivers. Collapses against me. Pulls my hair, screaming. "Fuck me, Deck. I can't stand it anymore. Please baby."

"Honey," I groan. "I love you so much. Did I ever tell you that?"

Her lips press my ear. "Tell me again. Show me."

"I love you, Johanna. More than anything. You're mine, baby. All mine." I knead the cheeks of her firm ass, lift and sling her legs around my hips.

"Tell me you're mine. You'll never do this with anyone but me."

I don't wait for an answer. I sink into her heat. She burrows her face into my shoulder and bites. Digs her fingernails into my back. Moans and groans.

There's nothing between us but water and glossy skin.

"I love you, Deck," she groans and rides me like there's no tomorrow.

While our bodies slip, I guide her ass, pound her again and again until I'm raw. Groaning, she sinks her nails deeper into the flesh of my back so fiercely, I think she's broken the skin. If not for the steady stream of shower, I'd be breaking a sweat.

Her heat clutches me like a tight fist, the

muscles lining her channel working overtime. "Christ, baby. You feel so good. Squeeze tight, baby, so I don't have to move. Let your body do incredible things to me." I'm so stoked, I feel like I'm suffocating.

When I ram harder, deeper, she gasps, collapses in my arms. My cock jerks and explodes, flooding her with my pent-up ecstasy.

"Holy Christ." I whistle an exhale as we slump to the tiled floor in silence: chests heaving, holding onto each other. "Nothing will ever separate us."

"Nothing." She repeats.

***

We're wrapped in robes. Johanna is curled up on the sofa. I light a fire, grab some cushions, and pull her onto the floor beside me.

"Come on, baby. Cuddle with me. Watch the flames lick the logs. It's relaxing."

"I don't need to be relaxed." She sinks against me. "I'm exhausted."

I let out a throaty laugh. "So much for skiing." I tug a fistful of her hair and draw her cheek to mine. "The day is shot."

"So is your load. Or were there two?" She laughs. Gazes at me with amazement. Contentment. "You're one wild man." She pokes my chest. Slides her palm down my biceps. "I've never seen you this way. We're going to have to come up here more often."

"Take me off the streets and this is what you get." I graze my cheek against hers, like kittens do. "I guess I held back at home. Didn't want to scare you away." I twist the belt of her robe between my fingers. Drag the tip over her legs that are stretched out before her. "I don't open up very easily."

"Don't hold anything back. You'll never scare me away. I think I know you better than you realize. It's all in those dreamy brown eyes." She urges my lids closed with her lips, dropping kisses on my lashes.

While I hold Johanna in my arms, beyond the window, the sun takes a nosedive into a sea of mist, but there's no sea. Only mountain ranges. While daylight finally fades, the moon tries to rise but presents only one side, the other half hidden by dusky clouds.

"Looks like that storm is blowing in. We'll be hitting the slopes tomorrow for sure. That sky looks like it's gonna dump five feet of snow tonight."

She shivers. "The sky can fall for all I care. I'm happy to be here with you." Her stare sinks into mine. "You make me feel safe, Deck. So loved." She slips a hand beneath my robe, dribbles her fingertips across my thigh. "Listen to that wind. It's pounding on the windows. It's creepy."

I crush her against my chest. "The only storm you have to worry about is the one in me." I tilt her face to mine, drag my lips from her chin to her forehead. "I don't know what I'd do without you, Johanna."

"Aww." She takes my face in her hands. Kissing the tip of my nose. "You never have to worry about that. I'll always be your prisoner." She smiles. Then her brows pull together, and her gaze grows intense. "I do worry about you though, working those streets." I feel a shudder ripple through her. "Busting drug deals and all ..."

"Honey. I'm a big boy." I tuck a lock of hair behind her ear. Run my fingertip across her chest, gently press the pad of my thumb into the hollow of her throat, followed by my lips that glide up her neck to nibble her ear. "Those goons know better than to mess with me." I draw back and wink. She's gorgeous. Hair cascading, eyes sparkling. Lips still puffy from mine. "I worked up a hell of an appetite. How about you, babe?" I tap the tip of her nose.

She nods. Tugs my bottom lip with her teeth. "I'm starving." She stretches with contentment. Her lazy sigh fills me with satisfaction. Swells my heart inside my chest that aches with love for this girl. How I'm going to handle this, I have no clue. Ask her to marry me? Holy fuck. The gritty detective taking a bride? Wait until the news spreads around the precinct.

I squeeze her thigh. "Come on, sweetheart. Let's throw some clothes on. Run down to the lounge and have some dinner, before the place closes. Bring a bottle back with us. Then I'll show you my rough side." I growl into her hollow behind her ear.

She brings her brows together. Threads her fingers through my hair. The glint in her crystal blue eyes is enlivening.

My dick begins to rise.

She lifts a brow and smirks. "If that was your gentle side, heaven help me."

The Angel

"What is this? The sixth night you've barged into my room?" I mumble, groggy, drunk with the need of sleep ... of her. Not that I mind opening my blurry eyes to the vision of an angel ... but Christ ... it's five a.m. and I have one hell of a hangover. My brain cells are literally slamming against my skull; what I did last night is beyond me. I have no freaking memory. One thing for certain, if I'd been with this luscious creature, I'd be feeling more than pain right now. At the thought, my morning wood expands.

I catch her movements from the corner of my eye, so I roll over to watch her, sink deeper into luxury. The cool satin bed sheet sweeps my erection like a soft palm ... hers. *Is something coming back to me?* Hell, she moves like a willow in a breeze, arching her back, stretching her limbs, purring sexy notes that spread wildfire through my veins.

Her skin glistens like she's wearing a sequin body stocking, but from my vantage point, I doubt she's wearing anything at all. Just pure crotch-stretching sex. Her skin is taught, creamy caramel ... mouthwatering. Despite the pounding head on my shoulders, I'm ready to devour every inch of her. I run my tongue across my lips. Prop on an elbow. Lift an inviting brow.

"Hey sweetheart. So what's your story?"

My cock is pulsing in time with the racehorse inside my chest that must be my heart, but I don't feel loving or romantic. Just freaking horny. I run a hand over my bulging crotch, groan with sweet pain. I need to slide inside that tantalizing opening ... now. I'm thinking she must be reading my thoughts, then I catch her examining gaze and my erection taps my belly.

A long tapered finger beckons me. I may feel like shit, but I'm ready for a seven day wonder. Yeah, that's right, by tomorrow we'll be perfect mates ... forever. I want to blow out a breath, figure out what's going on.

Mystified, I attempt to study her from head to toe, but I can't tear my eyes from her face. Sure, I love T & A just as much as the next guy, but I guess you could call me an *eye man*, because along with a succulent pussy, I love plunging into a woman's soul. And since the eyes *are* the soul, mine are stuck on the sultry stare of this gorgeous creation who is in the process of me even harder, if that's possible, as she curls around the foot of the bed.

I voice my confusion. "Who put you up to this?" I'm thinking one of the guys from back home is playing a prank and arranged this. "Did room service send you?" Christ, she's got my head in the clouds.

Her irises are like the holly decorating the room, the color of blood, trimmed with forest green. I've never seen anything like them before, and she doesn't remove them from mine as she slips a curious hand beneath the sheet. Her head tilts seductively from side to side. Her lips are pouty and pink, but sealed tightly shut. I wonder if they'd part for me. Mental note: pry them open with your tongue, maybe your dick. I know I sound gross, but she's got this magic going on. A power over me like I'm a puppet and she's controlling the strings. I'm helpless. Christ, what would Johanna say if she saw me now. *Johanna.* Where are you? This seraph's presence is wiping my scribbling mind cleaner than an eraser on a chalkboard.

Gripping my toes, she begins a sensual massage: first the balls of my feet, then the arches, working her way up my aching calves. The gap between my muscular legs widens. My balls clench. I choke out a sigh, permit my lids to drop, and let myself tumble.

Struggling for balance, my body swivels and bends, but I can't stop the momentum. My ears ring with the sound of a gunshot, blood thunders through my brain. The mountain echoes and heaves. Mind whirling, I reach out for her, but she's just beyond my fingertips. Then she's gone. I'm buried. Can't breathe.

Next thing I know, the thrilling touch of my bedside companion is groping its way up the inside of my thighs, fingernails raking, soft tips palpating. Holy shit. This woman could breathe on me and I'd come. My sack aches so bad, my orgasm is an inch away from blowing, like that mountain ... mountain?

My eyes cling to Johanna's face. Cheeks all rosy. Ruby red lips pursed. Not only is she wrapped in a furry white parka, but she's playful as the angora kitten she resembles; stumbling ten steps ahead of me, laughing, turning to bombard me with handfuls of powdery snow.

"Glad I talked you into coming up here?" Panting, I tackle her. In a lover's clutch, we sink onto a blanket of fresh fallen snow. The sky above reminds me of goose feathers. Clusters of gray clouds flock in high winds appearing just about ready to dump a blizzard on every square foot of this ski town.

Johanna giggles with delight, her warm breath a soft plume in frigid air. "I'm having the time of my life." Her lips come down on mine. Despite the dreary weather, they're soft and warm. I taste cocoa, cream, sweetness as her tongue sweeps mine.

When she lifts her lips she frowns. "Honey. When you were in the shower this morning, I got another message ..."

My blood begins to boil. I roll her off my chest, hold her at arm's length. The fear she's feeling shoots through me like a bolt of electricity heading straight to my gut. "That fucking stalker again? What did he say?"

Some guy's been hounding Johanna. Texting her. Leaving messages on her cell phone. Traceable, sure, but not without a battery in the phone. So far, I have been unable to track the bastard. He better hope I never find him. If I do, do I arrest him? Nah, kick his ass first, then send whatever's left of him to the slammer. No one messes with my baby.

"He never says anything. He just breathes into the phone. The air vibrating in his throat rattles, hisses like a snake. It's awful. Gives me the chills." She buries her face in my neck. "I try to reason with him, but ..."

"Don't try to talk to him! There's no reasoning with a stalker. You'll just be turning the sick bastard on. He'll hear the fear in your voice. Just hang up."

I unzip my jacket and yank it open, press her cheek against my warm, bulky knit sweater. "Don't

*worry, baby. I'll take care of everything. No one's
gonna hurt you ... ever."*

The disturbing memory jolts me fully awake,
but I can't shake the fog from my head. My brain
is like a hunk of rock, dense, incapable of reason.

*Why is this strange chick in here? What does
she want? Why the fuck isn't she talking?*

I should be able to read her. In my profession,
I should have been able to nail that stalker. I'm an
NYPD detective, up at this ski lodge for a week
of fun and sex. Booze and Johanna. The only
problem is, I'm stuck in this freaking room with
no memory of how I even got here, and a beautiful
girl wearing nothing but wings. Is she dressed, or
undressed, for Halloween? With a painted face
and a killer body, she could suck the wind out of a
hurricane.

But I can't get my mind off Johanna. Where is
she? Did I leave her down in the lounge? Sitting
alone before the crackling fire? Looking
desperate? Looking for me? Why would I do that?
Holy fuck. Suppose that creep found out about
our spur of the moment interlude. Followed us up
here. The thought of voyeurism hits me. Last I
recall, Johanna and I were prancing around naked
in our suite, drinking wine. I fucked her up against
the wall. Did we have the drapes closed? That
bastard could have been outside filming us for all
I know. How fucking dumb could I have been.

I reach for the nightstand, checking for my
Glock. Let out a frustrated breath. My fingers slide

across the smooth surface, finding nothing but a strip of condoms. What the fuck have I been doing? The packets aren't open, so apparently nothing yet. But a dozen? What did I have planned? Despite the bewildering situation I find myself in, I have to laugh. Leave it me. You can take the whore off the street but not out of the cop.

I've been this way since I was a kid. A tattooed bad boy on a Harley. Abandoned like an unwanted pup. Picking up chicks. Fucking them. Dumping them. Then along comes Joanna. In three months, she's got me by the balls, on my knees, and I'm up here on the slopes trying to find myself. Find Johanna.

The angel knows how to handle a guy. Her massaging hands are on my back, rolling my athletic frame onto my side. Crawling up behind me. We're skin to skin. Damn, she's so fucking tempting. Spooning her smoking hot body against mine. Just being beside her, I break into a sweat. I want to ram her so bad. But I can't. So I slam my palm on her hand before she has a chance to grab my junk.

I twist my head over my shoulder. "So you want me to fuck you ..."

"Mmm," is all she says.

I'll play her game. "Before we fuck, I need to know what I'm dealing with. Is this a test?" My brain is short circuiting. Johanna, you bitch. I told you I'm all yours. If you've been fucking around, sending hookers up here to find out if you can trust me, I'll ...

I flip myself over, jerk angel's crotch against my pelvis. Look her in the eye and rock my hips a few times. She's shooting me this lazy stare, which is melting my resolve. She's so soft. Christ, I could come against her belly. I don't know what the hell is going down. My rocket is ready to launch. My brain is on fire. I have to take my aggression out on someone. And apparently, she's here of her own free will ... so why not take advantage of the unexpected opportunity? How do I know Johanna isn't with that asshole in another room. Fucking his brains out like she did mine before we left home. Just thinking about banging her in the shower sends a chill down my spine. Thinking of him drilling her causes my gut to knot. She's mine. Case closed.

My lips are close to angel's face. My fingers tighten around her slender arms. "I've got questions that need answers, baby. The door is locked and bolted. I have a feeling you've been here before. How do you keep getting into my room?" My voice is hoarse, coming from a throat so dry I can barely swallow. My skin is tingling.

Blinking, I stare into the colorful eyes of the amazing angel who slips from my grasp, starts doing this double-jointed cat crawl across the mattress, a low growl rising from her otherwise silent throat. She grazes my body with hers.

"Can you talk or what?" Fuck frustration. Now

I'm coming apart. "What are you up to? Why did you lock me in here?" I narrow my blurry eyes at her. My dick isn't the only thing stiff: my joints are frozen, limbs like lead. It's getting harder and harder to focus, to move. "Did you drug me?" Now I'm worried about waking up in a bathtub of ice, missing a kidney.

It takes all of my strength, but I shove her away, roll off the bed and onto my feet. Stalk around the room, holding onto walls because now I'm fucking dizzy. Ripping empty drawers open, searching for my belongings. Other than the condoms, the room is bare. No boots, no pants, no wallet, no keys, no fucking cigarettes.

My craving for nicotine only inflames my desire for this mysterious angel, girl, creature, whatever the hell she is. I don't give a damn. I'm an animal in heat and if I don't slide into her soon, I'm gonna crash through that barred window. Barred? I rush to the window, rattle the frame, try to lift the sash. Solid as a rock. Shit, no escaping this way. I stumble to the door. The bolts won't budge. What the fuck?

"Hey ... open the door. I want out of this. You hear me? I'm done playing games with you, bitch. Let me out or ..."

She's been shadowing me, tickle torturing my ass with her fingertips, grabbing my junk. Next thing I know, she steps in front of me, pins me to the wall, drags her smooth tongue over my cheek, then tongue-fucks my ear. Slides her hand between my legs and starts tugging. All in what's becoming nerve-wracking, what the fuck is going on, silence. So there's no way in hell I'd be able to release this load, even if I wanted to. Which I do, yet I don't.

Her sharp teeth graze my throat. Her free hand caresses my ass. Wait ... her rose colored eyes are now forest green. I run a testing finger over her lips. What the fuck am I dealing with? Some kind of mutant witch?

She slams her body against mine. Throws a leg around my hip and swipes my cock with her wet pussy. I'm using every last bit of energy to stand up, no less resist her. I can't fuck another girl. My heart belongs to Johanna, which means, so does my dick.

I grab the back of her head. Jerk her face to mine. "Are you someone from my past? Holding a grudge or something? Talk to me. We can work this out." I shake her shoulders, then drop my arms to my side.

Maybe she's deaf, I don't know. She wraps me in a bear hug, grinds us across the floor and to the bed. Tosses me around like I'm weightless. Hops onto the mattress beside me and drops to her knees, like she wants me to do her doggie style. This chick just doesn't get it. I tap her ass.

"Baby, you're beautiful and all, tempting as hell, but I just can't." At another time I'd be sinking deep inside her, pounding her onto another planet. But I'm taken. I might even ask Johanna to marry me. I can't believe I'm thinking this way.

She crawls up between my legs, her face in my junk, and her tongue licks fire across my entire groin, up my shaft. I don't know how much longer I can hold out. I'm in agony, ready to scream.

"Why are you taunting me? What the hell's going on?" I push her off, try to pull my thighs together, but by now, I've weakened pathetically.

How can you let this chick push you around like this? I disgust myself. She starts in again, playing with my erection. Shifting it, stroking it, wrapping the head with her tongue. She's got this way of sucking that's making me squirm. I want to peel off her fingers, her lips, but I can't, because the way she's tugging and licking is driving me insane. She's got moves new to even me, the king of sluts.

Head rolling side to side I'm groaning, dragging my hands through my hair. Ready to start tearing it out from the root. I feel like I've had this erection for a week. Can't imagine who I have, or maybe haven't fucked. Then her lips come down and she takes me all in. Her tongue probes the slit, then my rod slams the back of her throat.

Her mouth is like a pussy, warm, tight, wet and delightful. I strain to watch her, keep my eyes from closing. She shoves a hand in her crotch, and as her head moves like a piston, her hips rock. I'm trying to distinguish between our moans, because the sounds are guttural. I fist her hair. Guide her pace.

I close my eyes and see Johanna. Smell her. Taste her. "Suck me. Harder, baby. I've been waiting for this for so long." I'm a raving lunatic. My hips thrust. The muscles in my ass clench. I grab hunks of her hair, bury my face in it. "Oh baby. You're killing me."

The feeling is incredible. Rapture is working its way up my shaft. When her lips clamp down, my entire being reacts: my groin, my butt, my belly, all catch the beat, and I think I'm about to erupt and bleed.

A combo of pleasure and pain grips my expanding balls, hits my prostate, building into a throbbing ache I doubt I can control much longer. I need to release so bad, but can't because when I open my eyes, it's not Johanna. So I start begging. "Stop. I can't do this ..." Even my legs ache. It feels as though her fingers are inside me, pinching my prostate. Every nerve is firing signals and the sensation is so intense, a cry of agony is ripped from my throat.

"Johanna!" I scream, because that's who I see hovering over me. In the back of my mind, something is telling me, "It's not her!" I blink frantically. Roll my head from side to side. I can't look at this chameleon. She's freaking killing me. "What do you want from me? Where's the girl I came up here with?" She's got me whimpering like a wuss. I hurl her away.

The room is dank. A pungent odor, like rotten fruit and bitter wine, drifts with angel to the other side of the bed where she cartwheels to a stop, perches at the edge, head angled, chin lifted. Her wings coil around her upper torso, their agile flutter now and then baring slivers of tempting flesh I want to lick from here to eternity, or at least until my tongue dries up and falls off, like my dick is about to.

"You're driving me crazy!" I cradle my head, pound my temples. "Stop torturing me!"

Angel's eyes are no longer enough. My imagination is running as wild as my urges. I want to see it all ... I *need* to see every tantalizing inch of her, so I crawl to her side, rise to her height, carefully peel away something that feels like a feather boa, unveiling the most scrumptious pair of breasts I've ever seen. Round and set high on her chest. Ripe raspberry tipped. And I'm about to ravage them. I lick the sensation of a bubble of saliva from the corner of my mouth. Suck in a nipple. Almost come when she groans a deep, "Mmm."

Her smile is sultry. She shoves me away, cups her full breasts, and smashes them into my face.

"So you want to play games?" I growl. "You like it rough?"

She lifts a brow. Runs her tongue over her lips. Slides a finger into her opening. Arches her back and lets out a groan.

"Keep performing like this and I won't be worth much. I've got less than five minutes left inside me. Let me take the helm for a while. That's what you want, isn't it?"

After a heavenly moment, I capture her other budding nipple in my mouth, draw on it like a straw, nip it with my teeth. It instantly swells, molds to my palate. With the tip of my tongue I flick the tender blossom, teasing until a moan catches in her throat. "Should I stop?" I whisper hoarsely. "Or take you on a ride you'll never forget."

She arches her spine, confirming her desire with a groan that sounds like it's pulled from her core. But her lips remain sealed.

"Talk to me, sweetheart," I blow into her ear. "It's kind of weird screwing around with a girl who just grunts. I don't even know who you are. What's your name? Can you speak?"

She thrusts a hip into my junk. I'm throbbing like a finger slammed by a hammer. I clutch her other breast, squeeze a handful of delicious flesh, then slip my palm between her thighs. She's so wet, I want to bury myself inside her. Writhing, she yelps like a bitch in heat when I rub her clit. She bucks and turns, trying to mount me.

"Holy Christ," I mumble. A sinking sensation curls my toes. She's not in costume. Her wings are definitely growing through the skin on her back. "Get the hell off me! You're not human."

"I am what you want me to be," she conveys in a blood-curdling hiss.

Effortlessly, her wings display in a five foot spread, baring it all. Her smooth, hairless body is magnificent: swan neck, slender waist, graceful hips. And yeah, those delectable breasts just pointing as if daring my lips, my hands, my hardon to slip between them.

She lifts her head. Slams her eyelids shut. Draws in an asphyxiating non-breath, because her chest doesn't heave, then stiffens like a statue. Tosses her head, leaps across the bundled sheets and lands on top of me. In one sweeping motion, we're face to face, cheek to cheek, and she's chewing my earlobe, whispering, "Are you happy I let you talk me into coming up here?"

"Ah. She speaks." I smack her ass, flip her onto her back and straddle her. I slide my hands beneath her globes and lift. "Hold on ... roll that back. I invited you here?"

"Ah huh." She licks her lips. "I'm having the time of my life."

She's hit a nerve, triggered a flashback; I remember the words Johanna said to me when we were locked in each other's arms.

She's blowing my mind. And my mind says: don't think ... just bang her. What you do doesn't matter. You're dreaming. "If we're about to fuck, shouldn't we exchange names?" I drop my lips onto hers, slip my tongue inside her mouth and work it. I close my eyes, about to surrender.

"Mmm," she moans. "Fuck me. While you still have some life in you." She grabs my dick and pumps. Aims it for her drooling slit.

My hooded eyes spring open. There's

something disturbingly familiar about this seraph. No ... it's not her eyes. Johanna's are clear blue crystals. This angel's have turned murky, and her hair isn't shiny platinum either, but rather like clumps of silk in a cornfield in the dead of night with no moon.

I pull my brows together and squint. "I feel like I know you, yet I don't."

She rolls me over like a log, squats and gyrates. "I know who you are Deckard Driscoll." She throws back her head and lets out a screech that rattles the windows. Or is that wind?

Her teeth look like razors. Holy shit. Is she some kind of cannibal? I'm about to corral her, cuff her. What the fuck am I locked in here with? I panic and quickly scan the room. No handcuffs. No gear. What is this place? Four walls. Frosted windows. Or are they blackened by fog? Skylights overhead but I can't see anything on the other side of the glass. Just endless night. And I know the clock I looked at earlier read five a.m. Where the fuck is daylight?

"So." I pull back, drag a hand through my hair. I squeeze my eyes shut and concentrate ... trying to recover my senses, my sanity. "You know me. How come I don't know you?" I grab her neck and pull, so her head hovers over mine. Our eyes are fixed, our lips are parted. My tongue's getting ready to dive into her mouth, my dick into her pussy. I'm flexing my glutes, slapping my erection against her apex.

Colliding with her clammy skin coats me with a chill, but still, I'm in need ... I'm almost ready ... until my palms graze the scales on her back, replacing her wings. What am I holding? She looks like Johanna but feels like a reptile. I squeeze my lids tighter and let them snap open. Is it the haze seeping from beneath the door that obscures my vision? Or are her features morphing right before my eyes? I grip her shoulders, catch my balance. Throw her off, pull myself into a sit, and squint into her eyes again.

"Johanna?" I try to gasp but my lungs won't respond.

"Don't talk. Just fuck me," she growls. "I don't get this chance very often."

"What chance?"

"The chance to fuck an atoning."

"Atoning?"

"Stop asking questions." Her eyes roll up into her head. Now they're white marbles. Smoke clings to every curve of her body. "Shut up and do it, before the seventh night."

"Seventh night? What? Wait ... I can't ..."

Her body starts shuddering, flames lick her torso. I do a double-take. If this chick is for real, she's one hell of a magician. She's on fucking fire, still sitting here, arms reaching out for me.

"You can't?" Her laugh is brittle, like the remnants of her charred nipples.

"You looked so much like Johanna. Tasted like her ..." My head's spinning, my voice like gravel.

The lump in my throat literally pains thinking about the woman I came here to be with. The one I love with every ounce of my miserable being.

The thing at the edge of the bed sucks on her bottom lip, then bites down. "If you love her so much, how can you forget her so easily? Come to me so willingly?"

"I didn't come to you. You've been chasing me around this room. Mind-fucking me. Making me think you're Johanna."

"Don't you remember anything about us?"

"Us who?"

"Never mind just get on your back — and you'll find out what I'm talking about." She twists her mouth, runs her tongue across my lips, growling, "Fuck me."

"There's no way I'm about succumb to your mind-control, succubus."

She unlocks her legs from their clasp on my hips, fans her wings, dives to the other side, and lights on the marble post. She arches a brow and a scorched wing shudders across her chest, covering one drooping breast. "You were so ready to fuck me. Unfaithful man," she spits with disgust. "I almost had you." She pats a palm. "Right here."

My stomach knots. My eyes burn. The racehorse inside my chest is barely trotting. "Why are you torturing me?" Either I've gone blind or a nebulous cloud has just crashed through the window. Because I can't see a fucking thing. I smell something like fresh air, but still can't inhale it.

As fast as it's flooded the room, the fog lifts and my heart stops beating, not because her irresistible scent steals my breath, but because her eyes turn to ash and begin to smolder. With a look of defiance she unravels her wings. Beneath them are peeling layers of shriveled skin. Sagging, leather-like.

"What's wrong Deckard Driscoll?" Steam pours from her mouth, halos her balding head. "You can't remember anything?"

I must have been on one hell of a binge last night. I'm still asleep, or I'm dead and steeping in purgatory ... maybe in hell ... because the scene is too freaking bizarre. And it's real. This is really fucking happening. My temples throb. My balls ache. My mind? Forget my mind. I've already lost it.

The room oscillates, darkness falls. Angel is now a glowing outline at the foot of the bed, a gargoyle with a massive wingspan. The mind games this chick is playing are working a number on my heads. Both of them. I'm shrinking and swelling. Vibrating and shuddering.

An icy glow slices the room in half. I'm in a vortex of shimmering silver, blinking off flashes of light, ominous shadows. My mouth fills with the nauseating taste of copper. Its bitter taste rises from my tongue to my nostrils. My lids stretch, water runs from my eyes.

Despite the fact that beauty has transformed

into a beast, the pulse between my legs reminds me, if I don't release, I'll explode. She's got this magnetism. I'm an animal caught in a trap. Squirming, begging my keeper for release. Fuck this shit.

She shoots me a wicked grin. Her ember stare is deep, moody; hell yeah, she's my kind of bitch.

Johanna

When I come to, my naked ass is hanging off the side of the bed. I'm still holding the neck of the quart of bourbon either the carpet or I have consumed. The room is a vacuum, void of air. I lift a hand to my chest; it's cold, still. Christ, I'm suffocating. So I try to drag in a breath, inhaling booze, not oxygen.

I get a sense of a sweet spring garden. Then Johanna steps from a blinding light and floats into view. I know it's Johanna because her ivory skin is flawless and bare, except for the crimson rose tattoo blooming just above her luscious left breast.

There are two words for Johanna Kingston: Breathtaking magnificence. Her long blonde hair swirls around her shoulders. Cherry pink nipples play peek-a-boo through her curly locks. "Johanna?" I mumble, rubbing my balls. Wanting her so bad I think I'm about to die.

My abs crunch as I spring to a sit, too astounded to utter a damn word. My mouth must be hanging open because Johanna giggles as she approaches. She's carrying two scarlet goblets. Except for the red satin ribbon tied around her tiny waist, she's stark naked.

I reposition and groan. Rub my eyes. "Baby … you're here … you didn't …"

She glides to my side. Lowers her lovely bottom onto the mattress, and combs her fingers through my tangled hair. "Leave you?"

"Yeah. No, I mean …" I hold her at arm's length and glare. "Were you with that guy? Did you set me up? What the hell happened out there on the slope?" I'm so fired up, I don't know what to ask first. I want to grab her shoulders. Shake the truth out of her. I want to take her in my arms. Fuck her until she screams. Christ. I don't know if I can do any of it. I'm growing weaker by the minute.

Her ruby lips curve into an adoring smile, her whimsical laugh circles my head. She hands me a goblet. "Drink this. It will help."

"Wine?"

"Something like that."

My body is damp but chilled. I'm trembling. "Are we still out there, honey?" Things are beginning to come together. I try to suck in air, but there isn't any. "Baby ... are we?"

"Sip, Deck. Relax. It will all come back to you. Give it a moment." Her lips graze my cheek, her hand slides across my shoulder. One of her breasts presses my side. Her nipple is erect, arousing me. I wrap my arm around her, smoothing my fingers along her spine. My hand comes to a dead stop on her upper back, checking for wings. She feels so good, so warm, so real. Not like that mind-shattering dream.

My gaze shoots beyond Johanna's head, zeroing in on the wall of windows. Reality hits like the bolt of lightning piercing the glass. The odd thing is, the stunning flash is not entering the room, it's exiting.

There's nothing outside but wispy clouds. No mountains, no sky, no sun, no stars. No snowstorm.

"Where are we, Johanna?"

"In transition." Her hand slides up my thigh, massages my swelling shaft. "We don't have much time, Deck. If you want to be with me forever, we have to make love ... like we've never made love before."

Seriously? My eyes bulge. I gulp the fruity drink, drop the goblet on the floor. "Come to daddy." I pull her onto my lap. She squirms into place, charging every nerve in my body with electricity. My hardness presses against her firm ass. I grip her hips, slide her back and forth, stoking the fire in my groin. "Holy shit, baby. I need you so bad. Where have you been?"

"All you need to know is that I love you," she whispers, running her tongue around my ear. "Now fuck me."

"I love you more, and I'm about to fuck your brains out." I run my index finger over the rose on her breast, followed by my lips, then stare up at her. "You weren't here earlier, were you?"

She laughs softly. "That wasn't me, babe."

"You know about her?" My eyes strain, then narrow. "Did you send her?"

She gazes intently. "You called her."

"I called her?" I can't make heads or tails of what she's saying, which makes the room begin to spin.

I'm losing control. I'm crawling on the ceiling, my back is slamming against the walls. My fingers and toes are suction cups. I'm sticking to the window like some kind of alien creature.

"Who was she ... it ... whatever ..."

Johanna scruffs my head, like I'm the little boy I feel like right now. "The angel of death."

If I could let out a *phew,* I would. "Angel? Devil is more like it."

"One in the same, Deck."

Now I know exactly what the demon bitch meant by *us* and my body starts to shake.

My mind flies into reverie. My life flashes before me like a speeding train on an endless track. Memories: good, bad, beautiful. Years pass and I focus on Johanna, who looks so sweet and fresh, young and vulnerable.

"Remember the first day we met?" I thread my fingers through her hair, bury my face in a handful. Her hair smells fruity, something like my drink.

Johanna grins. Eases me back onto the bed. Crawls up beside me and burrows under my arm. One of her legs crosses mine. "How could I forget? You answered the door in your briefs." She giggles, pushes a lock of hair behind her ear. "Almost gave me heart failure."

"That bad, huh?"

"That good." Her fingers trace my abs, plucking the tufts of hair crossing my pecs. "The first thing that hit me was your muscular chest. The tribal art." Her touch explores the patterns climbing to my neck. She circles my triceps. "The black ink rippling with your muscles is such a turn on. I couldn't help but wonder how your strong arms would feel around me." She trembles. "The things you could do to me. We could do to each other."

"Oh, baby." My lips slide up and down her neck. "You smell so good. Kind of like the day we met."

"Mmm. You smell spicy." Her tongue flicks across my nipple which hardens instantly.

"You were an hour early." When she tosses her face up to gaze at me, I brush stray wisps of long bangs from her lashes. I drink in the sight of her, can 't keep my hands off her. But I lie beside her and stare in amazement, because she's all mine.

"I have a confession to make. I knew who you were Detective Driscoll, so when your request for a quote came into the office, I called first dibs."

"How'd you know who I was?"

"Your reputation preceded you."

"Huh?"

She laughs. "I saw you in a bar one night when I was with friends. You busted this girl's boyfriend. I heard all about it ... and about you."

I drag a hand over my face. Groan. "Bad shit ..."

"No. Amazing. I think I fell in love with you that night. The way you leaned against the bar, so careless, arrogant actually. Shoulders squared, hip cocked. The way you pursed your lips, slugged down shots. So masculine. So hot. You had a hard look in your eyes, but I knew inside here." She taps my chest. "A good heart was beating."

I'm overcome. I want to cry, but can't find tears. "Why didn't you come over to talk to me?"

"I walked right by you ... slowly. But you looked right through me." She wrinkles her nose. "I'll never forgot those dreamy eyes that seemed to be looking everywhere, but nowhere. Like you had the weight of the world on your mind."

"I was probably drunk on my ass, otherwise I would have done this." I draw her into my arms and press my lips to hers. Our kiss is sweet, like Johanna. "Holy shit. I'd never forget that ass." I palm my forehead. "That was *your* ass wiggling out the door." I reach behind and pinch her. "I knew there was something familiar about these cheeks."

"That was me." She giggles. "We hung around in the parking lot afterward. I saw you leave. My eyes were glued to your ass-hugging jeans."

I shake my head. "You're kidding."

She props on an elbow. Circles my mouth with her pinky. "Nope. You sauntered over to your bike like you owned the place, then took off like a bat out of hell. Never looked back once." She tilts her head and her hair swings over her shoulder, draping the lacy pillow. "I wondered what your story was." She kisses my temple, then taps it. "What was going through this gorgeous head."

"Probably nothing." I laugh, but when I catch the look on her face my lips freeze. Want to tremble. The love in her eyes is like a haymaker. If there was air in my lungs, it would be knocked out of me. "I was just biding my time, babe."

"I figured you were taken. Maybe married."

My fingers slice through her gleaming curtain of hair, uncovering her ear. "I was waiting for you," I whisper.

"How fate brought us together ... brought us here." Her facial muscles tighten, then release.

"Who knew an inquiry for an insurance quote would lead to this." I chuckle. Pull her tighter. Hold her like I never want to let her go. I run my fingers softly up her thigh. "That first day I saw you at my door, standing there holding a briefcase. I knew I was a goner." I tweak her nose. "You looked like a little girl trying to pass for a grownup." I can't hold back a belly laugh.

"And I got to stare into your irresistible brown eyes again." Her fingertips sweep the side of my face, followed by a flurry of kisses. "I instantly fell in love with your eyes, among other things." She giggles, lays her palm on my cock which is bouncing her hand.

"You. All dressed in a business suit. I had no idea you'd change my life. That I'd turn a one eighty ... willingly. You know, other women tried, unsuccessfully."

"Don't I know it." She gazes up at me and the love in my heart is even stronger than the heat between my legs.

"You've always been the only one, Johanna."

"We ended up in your bedroom." She flushes. "I couldn't believe I let that happen."

"Honey, with the draw between us, it was inevitable." Smiling, I sink into the memory. "I felt like I was going to bed with a high school girl, which made our first time even hotter."

"I've been told I have a baby face. I won't age ..."

"Yeah, and a woman's body that would make any guy drool himself dry, but you're mine." My eyes burn into hers. "Tell me."

"What? That you bought the most expensive life insurance policy? Five million." She wraps a finger with a chunk of my hair. "I got some crazy commission. You supported my shopping sprees single-handedly."

"Forget about commission. Tell me you're mine. And always will be."

She brings her lips to my cheek and murmurs, "I'm yours, forever."

"So, who's gonna collect on that policy?" I laugh. "Since you're my beneficiary and we're both here. What happens with the cash?"

"The company gets to keep it."

"Figures." I tickle her nose with a lock of her hair. "Who needs money. I've got you." My lips brush her shoulder. "It feels like we've been together forever, babe."

"When you touch me, it feels like the first time. I'll never tire of you."

"Well that's good to know since we're about to share eternity."

I stare into the crystal blue eyes of the woman I so desperately adore. I want to be with for the rest of my ... my what? Death?

My jaw tightens. Nothing ... no one is going to take her away from me. Not the stalker. Not the fucking angel of death.

"So, if the clock is ticking, why are we wasting time talking?" My gaze runs over her breasts, followed by my fingers. I draw a line down the valley between her abs, zero in on her sweet, slick crotch. Her skin is cold as ice, but the swell between her legs is unbelievably warm. I circle her clit with a finger, and her hips automatically rock.

"You tell me ..." Her growl is soft, not menacing like the angel's. Not abrasive like mine. Johanna is pure. Love. Beauty. Dead? I still can't come to terms with it.

"Any chance I'm dreaming this?"

"Na ah." She licks my ear. Tickles my balls with a teasing touch. "There's no getting away from it. We're really here, Deck. This is what people wait their entire lives for."

"Christ. You sound excited," I grumble.

"I am." Her round eyes widen, sparkle.

I grab a handful of her silky platinum hair, and we tumble across the sheets. Side by side we gaze into each other's eyes. A strange feeling overtakes me, like I'm being cleansed. I have to make a full confession or I'll never be at peace. "Before we make love, I need to get something off my chest. I wasn't attracted to her ..." I stammer. "She had this obscene power over me. I was in the palm of her hand." I don't mention I'm referring to my junk. "I swear, I would never have ..."

"Shh." Johanna says as her arms wind around my neck. "Stop explaining, Deck. Nothing matters. It's just you and me now."

"This is gonna be amazing," I mumble against her nipple that's stuffed in my mouth. "I think I hear harps. But where are the pearly gates everyone talks about?"

I'm wondering how we're going to get through those gates, if there are in fact, pearly white gates. Maybe it's all a fairy tale. Maybe we've never lived. We're an experiment in some Petrie dish and some computer is feeding us with thought. Maybe we've been dead all along and are just coming to life now. The stuff streaming through my head is incredible. Weird. Mind-boggling.

Any way you cut it, with the life I've led, the immoral act I almost took part in with the dark angel, I'm fucked. Shit, I don't deserve eternal peace. A crooked cop, taking bribes. Never went to Mass, didn't believe in anything more than getting ahead in life, any way I could. For everything I've done I should burn.

Johanna breaks my thoughts, thank Christ, because if my heart was beating, it would be up and out my throat by now.

"Patience, my pet. You'll see what's in store for you." Johanna's smile lights up her face. She's always had the most beautiful smile. Did I appreciate what I had? I slam my fists into my forehead. If I could point the barrel of the Glock to my temples, instead of my fingers, I'd ... Who the fuck am I kidding? My mind's already been blown to bits.

Now I'm really panicking. The woman I love is obviously about to soar with the angels. I'm going to one place. She's on her way to another. How can I exist without her?

"Johanna, I wasn't going to do her. I swear, baby. I don't know why, but I thought that bitch was you. She cast a spell over me. I was so fucking horny I couldn't think straight. She spread her wings and all I saw was pussy."

Johanna frowns, then a twinkle fills her eyes. "I know, Deck. She's powerful. And you're just a man." She gives my balls a playful squeeze.

"Yeah. A sex starved man who's about to fuck the woman he loves more than life." I nuzzle her neck, slide my tongue around her ear. "What's with the ribbon?"

"Let's just say I earned one stripe for good behavior." Her smile fades into melancholy.

"Oh yeah? What were you, Santa's good little helper?" I run my palm across her clit while I suckle her neck. Twist her nipples with the fingers of my free hand.

Her body arches, then tenses.

Her words against my throat are muffled. "I was murdered. That counts for something."

"Oh, Christ, Johanna." I pull my fingers from her crotch, slam her body against me. "I'm sorry, baby. I didn't mean to crack jokes. I had no idea." With her head buried against my chest, I stare up at the skylights, seeing nothing but a swirling dark mass. "I wanted to protect you, and I let you get murdered." A sob tears from my throat.

She cradles my head. Brushes her fingers through my hair. "You tried to save me, Deck. You jumped in front of me to take the bullet, but you slipped on ice. You were ready to give up your life for me. Then that mountain came crashing down on us."

"Avalanche?" I remember the roar. Turning

in horror to see the white wave heading straight for us. I tried to grab Johanna, but even though I moved in what felt like slow motion, it all happened so fast. There was nothing I could do. I can't remember the exact moment of impact. Or how it felt. I just remember freezing. If hell is cold, maybe I was there.

"Oh, honey. Did you suffer? Was it over quickly?" I fight for air. "I barely have any memory of it."

"No. It didn't hurt, Deck, and yes, it was over in a heartbeat. One minute we were laughing, deciding what to eat for dinner. Kissing." Her eyes glisten. "You proposed to me." She grins. Wrinkles her nose. "Can you believe it? You said, and I quote, *I'm about to throw in the towel, Johanna. How long have we known each other?*"

"Romantic, huh." I hide behind my hands.

Her smile fades. Her fingers bite into my shoulders. "You were saying everything I wanted to hear. And the next minute ..." Her gaze carries concern. "Stop gasping. There's no air here. We don't need it."

"It was the stalker ..."

She nods. Chews her bottom lip.

"Did they catch the bastard?" My teeth clash, because my jaw clenches so hard. "If I could've gotten my hands on him. We wouldn't be here like this. If only I could have ..."

"Don't beat yourself up. What's done is done. It was fate. This is the way it's supposed to be,

Deck. And you had to go through this, blind. You'll understand." Her mouth pulls grim. Her face shadows as if the memory is fresh and painful. "He's still at the bottom of the mountain, covered with snow. They may never find his soulless body."

"I hope he burns in hell."

"He already is." She buries her face in my chest, then lifts her eyes to mine.

She winces. Chews harder on her lip. "I'm compelled to be honest, Deck." Her gaze shifts to the windows. Outside the fog begins to lift. Beams of light prism the room with brilliant colors.

My dead heart wants to break into a gallop. "You knew him, didn't you." I guess I knew it all along but couldn't face it, and right now, can't disguise the scowl. Restrain the mounting anger.

"Until he turned into a monster, yes." She lowers her head, then her eyes work their way to mine. "Please don't look at me that way. I never meant to hurt you. It only happened once. Remember the Bahamas trip the company sent me on?" She sounds like a scared little girl. "He was my boss. I knew him long before you, Deck. We ... He wanted ..."

"Don't. I don't want to know." I shake my head, bury my face in my hands.

She frees my face, forcing me to look at her. "When we got back, he wouldn't leave me alone. He threatened to tell you."

"So you kept fucking him," I growl. Grab a

fistful of her hair. Pull her face an inch from mine. All I want to do is kiss her.

"I told him I couldn't see him anymore. That I was completely in love with you." The truth is in her eyes. I believe her.

"Did they find us out there?" I shiver.

"They will." She nods.

"They say hearing is the last sense to go. But I never stopped hearing you, Johanna. Seeing you." My laugh is forced. "Yeah, even in that shrew, all I saw was you."

"Which is why she left, and I was able to enter. Had you given into her, you'd be with her right now." She shudders. Burrows closer into my side. "The thought is so frightening." She tilts her face to mine. Her voice strains. "I had to watch it. Wonder if you were strong enough."

I remember the sensation of voyeurism, and cringe. "So watching me was your punishment."

"And being taunted sexually was yours." With a finger, she lifts my dick and lets it thump against my belly. "You had me worried there for a while."

I roll my eyes, nuzzle her ear. "So we both fucked up."

"And we both atoned."

"It's that easy?"

"Yes it is. As easy as fighting temptation. You didn't finish, Deck." She looks like she's about to sigh, but her beautiful breasts don't heave. "Had you ejaculated, we wouldn't be here right now. Despite the temptation she threw at you, you held it together. For me. In the end, you saved both of us." She lowers her brows. Scrunches her mouth. "We're gonna make it, Deck." She nods, then smiles. "We were meant to be together. In our past life, and the one we're about to start."

I roll from the bed, pull Johanna down beside me. Face to face, we sit on the floor, asses buried in thick red carpet. We don't talk, we simply gaze. The electricity flowing between us is more powerful than her transgression. And hell, she paid the price with her life ... and mine.

Even though she's atoned, I can't believe Johanna cheated on me. I have to take my frustration out on something ... someone. I'm still not completely purged of humanity. As they say, old habits die hard. Kind of like I'm doing.

"It's not easy for me." I grit my teeth. "Letting go of life is a bitch. So is accepting your infidelity."

"I know, baby." Johanna has a pleading look on her face. "Time is running out. We have to hurry. I'll make it up to you." She's on her knees, lowering her face into my crotch. Whispering, "I'm going to suck you and fuck you until you *want* to die."

"Not if I do you first." I lift her face, swing her around, toss her over the side of the bed and grab her hips. Run my palms over her ass cheeks. Nothing feels like Johanna.

I slide my arms around her waist and up her body from behind, cupping her breasts. Roll her nipples between my fingers. The downward slide of my palms is caught by the ribbon which is still in place. I untie it, lift her arms above her head, bind her wrists, and finish the knot with a red satin bow.

I run my hands down her sleek, naked body, my fingers stalling on the soaked spot between her legs. My fingers plunge. Wiggle. I pull her ass up into position. Tease her with the tip of my erection. I've never felt anything so slick.

"What should I do to you now?" I rock into her.

"I should be punished, Deck. I was so bad." She grinds against me. Lets out a guttural growl.

Something shiny grabs my attention: a brass hook hanging low from the vaulted ceiling. I have no idea why it's here, but as long as it is, I'm gonna put it to good use.

I slap Johanna's smooth behind. "Appropriate punishment is coming right up."

I pull her to her feet and spin her around. Hoist her over my head. Hang her bound wrists over the hook, then step back and watch her dangle. I feel my heat expand.

"Deck! What are you doing?" Her body twitches.

"Shush. The punishment fits the crime, my love."

Her head hangs to her shoulder. Her eyes lower. She bites the side of her bottom lip.

"I'm going to tongue-fuck you, baby. Do you with my fingers. Then my bulging cock. Stop every time you're about to come. You'll beg me to finish you off. But I won't," I snap. "Do you know why?" I soothe my thudding rod with my palm. If I could breathe, I'd be gasping.

"Tell me," she groans.

"Because there's pleasure in pain. And you're about to experience both, simultaneously."

I lick my lips with anticipation. Wrap her legs over my shoulders, so my nose is buried in her folds. I flick her clit with the tip of my tongue, then clutch the slippery pearl with my lips and suck. She moans and thrashes. My tongue plunges through her slit, driving her to frenzy. At the onset of each climax, I grudgingly back away, disregarding her pleas. "I have to teach you a lesson, Johanna."

"Fuck me now, Deck. You cruel bastard."

Still clinging to my own life, I imagine her to be gasping. I dig my nails into her ass. Slap her swell against my face, then lift her off the hook. Her body slowly slides down mine. She whimpers as I fling her over my shoulder, toss her carelessly onto the bed.

"Are you ready for rough?"

She struggles against the bindings. "Untie me. I want to touch you." Her wrists are as red as the ribbon. Her tangled hair covers half of her face.

"No touching. I'm gonna pound your pussy until you scream for mercy."

"Fuck me with your huge cock."

She stretches out invitingly, but stares up at

me with uncertainty. A shudder ripples through me. I grab her ankles and drag her to the edge of the mattress.

Johanna is on her back, arms extended over her head. Her helpless expression is in one word: exciting. She stares up at me as if I'm her savior. The her mouth goes slack, silently begging for my kiss.

I spread her legs. My knees drop onto the mattress. Bracing an arm on either side of her head, I allow my hips to slowly fall. Our lips are inches apart. I slide my nose along her sculpted jaw line. Draw back to watch passion claim her face. Desire cloud her eyes.

My throbbing erection rhythmically grazes her sweet spot. "How bad do you want me?"

She tosses her head from side to side. Licks her bottom lip. "So bad."

"Bad enough to die for me?"

Her eyes bore into mine. Our bodies are on fire, yet our skin is dry.

"Yes," she whispers. "I'm ready to die for you."

I ram every inch of my heat into her; the thrust of her hips lifts my ass into the air. She squeezes her eyes shut. Buries her face against my arm. Sucks on my wrist, then bites it.

"Deck ..." she screams. "I love you." With each toss of her head, her hair whips her face.

I brush away the long strands covering her sultry eyes.

We pump and grind. Groaning, she takes a mouthful of the sheet that's bunched up around us. I pull it from her lips, jerk her face up. Crush her mouth with mine. The room falls eerily silent. No whispers. No heavy breathing. No creaking mattress. I swipe her neck with my tongue, lower my face, suck her hardened nipples.

"In a minute you'll be mine, forever."

There isn't a sliver of space between us. I grasp her hips and pound.

The force of my passion jolts Johanna across the bed, until her head hangs over the side. I take the weight with my hand. I'm ready to explode, but my body goes rigid.

"I can't, Johanna ..." My eyes flash around the room. "Don't you understand?" Panic fills my voice. "Once I do, everything will end."

"No, baby. Don't worry. This is how it's always going to be," she whispers. "Come baby. You can finally let go."

My being fills with fear, anger, pain. But when I look into Johanna's eyes, nothing matters. I'm safe. I'm home. I unleash her wrists and her arms fold around me.

The giant fist holding my gut is twisting and as we move together the contractions come in incredible waves. My vision blurs. I can't control my body. I'm floating. Crashing. Caving. I arch my back and clench my toes because I'm finally able to come. I grit my teeth and groan. My body jerks with spasms. I can't stop my muscles from straining. I almost lose consciousness, the pleasure is that intense. I feel like I'm dying. And I am. Or I have. Whichever it is, it's amazing.

I grab a fistful of Johanna's hair and squeeze. She's still clutched by an orgasm. Raking her nails down my back. Watching the passion on her face causes me to harden again. This is incredible. It's like one continuous fuck fest. But we're not simply fucking. We're making love.

For a split second everything makes sense. I know who I am. The reason I'm here. I'm with the woman I'll love for eternity. An otherworldly burst of energy passes between us. The naked vulnerability is overwhelming. We're actually sharing our souls. And it's beautiful.

"Johanna," I choke, "you're mine. Forever." I'm drained by a rush of drowsy hormones, but ready for another euphoric orgasm. "No stalkers, no time clocks. No worry. No fear."

Johanna's plush lips come down on mine. We wrestle across the mattress, tangling in the sheets, mating like two demons on their way to heaven.

About The Author

Lana Lundon is new to the world of literary erotica. Because she still believes in fairy tales, she has decided to pick up a pen and create her own. She spends most of her time imprisoned in her Pacific Northwest mountain chalet with her vibrator, waiting for her prince to walk magically through the electric fence and climb her trellis. Which is why she never locks her bedroom window, and sleeps in the nude. *Seven* is her first attempt at erotic fantasy. She hopes to write more stories and gain a fan base. The idea of sharing her fantasy work with others makes the creating process even more exciting. Despite her reclusive tendency, Lana loves to communicate with the outside world via email and through her blog.

http://lanalundon.blogspot.com/